Susan and Gordon Adopt a Baby

Based on the
Sesame Street television scripts
by **Judy Freudberg** and **Tony Geiss**

Illustrated by **Joe Mathieu**

Featuring the **Sesame Street** characters
and the Sesame Street cast:
Linda Bove as Linda
Northern Calloway as David
Emilio Delgado as Luis
Loretta Long as Susan
Sonia Manzano as Maria
Bob McGrath as Bob
Roscoe Orman as Gordon
Miles Orman as Miles
Alaina Reed as Olivia

Random House / Children's Television Workshop

Copyright © 1986 Children's Television Workshop. Sesame Street puppet characters © 1986 Jim Henson Productions, Inc. All rights reserved under International and Pan-American Copyright Conventions. ® Sesame Street and the Sesame Street sign are trademarks and service marks of the Children's Television Workshop. Published in the United States by Random House, Inc., New York, and simultaneously in Canada by Random House of Canada Limited, Toronto, in conjunction with the Children's Television Workshop.

Library of Congress Cataloging-in-Publication Data:
Freudberg, Judy. Susan and Gordon adopt a baby. SUMMARY: Big Bird tries hard to be helpful when a new baby arrives on Sesame Street. [1. Babies—Fiction. 2. Adoption—Fiction. 3. Puppets—Fiction] I. Geiss, Tony. II. Mathieu, Joseph, ill. III. Henson, Jim. IV. Children's Television Workshop. V. Sesame Street (Television program) VI. Title. PZ7.F88983Su 1986 [E] 86-2951 ISBN: 0-394-88341-1 (trade); 0-394-98341-6 (lib. bdg.)

Manufactured in the United States of America   10 9 8 7 6 5 4

Big Bird was roller-skating down Sesame
Street when he saw Susan and Gordon taking lots
of big boxes out of their car.

"Hi, Susan! Hi, Gordon! What's in the
boxes?" he asked.

"Hi, Big Bird," said Gordon. "This is
furniture and other things for Miles."

"Miles? Who is Miles?" asked Big Bird.

"The baby!" said Susan as she and Gordon carried a crib box up the steps of their apartment house.

"Don't you remember, Big Bird?" said Gordon. "We told you about him. Susan and I are adopting a baby, and his name is Miles."

"Oh, right. I forgot," said Big Bird. "But what does 'adopting' mean?"

Gordon put the crib box down and looked at Big Bird. "Adoption is one of the ways a baby comes into a family," he said. "Susan and I want a child to love and take care of, so we're adopting Miles."

"Now he is our son," said Susan, "and we will be his parents forever."

Big Bird followed Susan and Gordon into their apartment.

"Gee," said Big Bird, "a baby on Sesame Street. I'll have a new friend! I'll have someone to roller-skate with! And we'll play ball and hide-and-seek and hopscotch."

Susan laughed. "Not right away, Big Bird. Miles is too little to do those things."

"Oh," said Big Bird. He was disappointed.

"But there are other things you can do with him," said Susan.

"Like what?" asked Big Bird.

"Well, you can tell him stories. And you can sing to him and introduce him to your teddy bear, Radar," said Susan.

"Oh, boy, I can hardly wait," said Big Bird. "When is this baby coming?"

"Tomorrow," said Susan.

"Tomorrow!" said Big Bird. "I'd better go home and start getting ready right now!"

The next day Big Bird and his friends waited on the steps of 123 Sesame Street for Susan and Gordon to bring baby Miles home. Olivia was ready with her camera to take pictures for Miles' baby album. Big Bird was ready with his ukulele, a storybook, a bag of blocks, and Radar.

Finally Gordon and Susan's car stopped in front of the house. Everyone crowded around Susan as she carried Miles up the steps.

"Oh, he is *so* cute!" cried Grover. Everyone agreed.

After everyone had said hello to the baby, Gordon said, "We have to take Miles inside now to change him."

"*Change* him?" asked Big Bird, shocked. "You just got him! Don't you like him?"

Susan laughed. "Gordon means we have to change Miles' diaper. We'll see you all later."

Then, as Susan was going inside, she noticed how sad Big Bird looked. So she said, "Big Bird, would you like to come inside and help us make Miles feel at home?"

Big Bird happily went inside with his ukulele and storybook and bag of blocks and Radar.

While Gordon changed the baby's diaper, Big Bird tried to show Miles the pictures in his storybook. "Look, Miles! There are the Three Little Pigs," said Big Bird.

"Would you please move, Big Bird?" asked Gordon. "I'm trying to change his diaper. Now is not a good time to read Miles a story."

Then Susan put Miles into his new highchair and began feeding him cereal. Big Bird stood next to the highchair, strumming his ukulele and singing loudly, "Sunny day, chasing the clouds away." Miles began watching Big Bird and not the little spoons of cereal that Susan held out for him.

"Big Bird," pleaded Susan, "I'm trying to feed the baby. Now is not a good time to sing to Miles."

After Miles ate his cereal, Gordon wanted to put him into a clean little snugglebunny suit. He had just begun to snap Miles into the suit when—*clunk!*—Big Bird dumped his wooden blocks onto the changing table next to the baby.

"Come on, Miles, let's build a castle!" Big Bird said.

Miles rolled toward the blocks.

"I can't dress Miles while he plays with blocks," said Gordon. "Not now, Big Bird."

Big Bird became very quiet for a moment. Then he said, "I'm going back to my nest. Miles can't play with me. And you're both so busy with him that you don't have any time left for me. I guess you don't have any love left for me either."

Gordon put his arm around Big Bird. "Oh, yes we do!" he said. "We don't run out of love. In fact, when a new baby comes to a family, the love just grows and grows so that there's enough for everyone."

Just then Miles began to cry.

"Please don't go, Big Bird," said Susan. "We need you to comfort Miles. Can you do something to cheer him up while I warm his bottle?"

"Well," said Big Bird, "Miles might like my hop-on-one-foot-with-my-hands-behind-my-back trick." And he tried it.

But Miles did not stop crying.

"Maybe he'd like my silly faces," said Big Bird. "Look at this, Miles. Yoo-hoo!"

"Don't move, Big Bird," said Olivia. "I've got to get a picture of this!" And just as she was ready to snap the picture, Miles stopped crying and smiled the biggest smile of his life.

"Big Bird," said Susan, "you make Miles so happy. Would you like to give him his bottle?"

So Big Bird sat in the rocking chair and held Miles and fed him the bottle of milk. He hummed a tune softly until Miles fell asleep.

"Good work, Big Bird," Susan whispered. "I'll put him in his crib now."

"Okay, Susan," said Big Bird. "I have to go now. I can't wait to tell Mr. Snuffle-upagus the good news. We have a baby on Sesame Street!"

"Here, Big Bird," said Olivia. "You can show Snuffy this picture."

Mr. Snuffle-upagus was just finishing his spaghetti and was about to take his nap when Big Bird arrived at his cave.

"Oh, Snuffy, did you hear the good news? There's a baby at Susan and Gordon's house!"

"Oh, really?" Snuffy yawned. "How long is he going to stay?"

"*Forever!* Susan and Gordon adopted him, and that means that he will be their son forever.